Get **more** out of libraries

Please return or renew this item by the last date shown.

You can renew online at www.hants.gov.uk/library

Or by phoning 0300 555 1387

Hampshire
County Council

Pip the Little Penguin

Roger Priddy

priddy books

For all little dreamers, wherever they may be

Illustrated by Lindsey Sagar
Based on original illustrations by Jo Ryan

This book was made by Mara van der Meer,
Penny Worms and Kate Ward.

Copyright © 2016 St. Martin's Press, LLC
Published by priddy☺books
53–64 Chancery Lane, London, WC2A 1QT
Text originally published as Rainbow Rob in 2006.

All photos credited to iStockPhoto: Aurora Borealis © Nikolay Pandev; Lily pads © cyoginan;
Baked beans © craigratcliffe; Single baked bean © Chris Elwell; Cotton candy © Darren Mower;
Pine cone © ivstiv; Coffee © Vinicius Ramalh Tupinamb; Popcorn © Coldimages; Wheat ears © gilas; Sand
texture © Milberra; Mashed potato © travellinglight; Football © Anthia Cumming; Hairbrush © alenkadr.

Pip is black and Pip is white,
just a normal penguin – dark and light.
But Pip does not like black and white.
He feels so dull. He wants to be bright!

Then one day...

Pip looked up at a light-filled sky.
He looked at his dad and he asked him why,
if there is red and green and blue...

"Can't little penguins be colourful, too?"

"I want to be **blue**, just like a whale –
a big blue whale with a big blue tail."

"Pip, you're not big
and you're just not blue.
You're black and white,
and quite small, too."

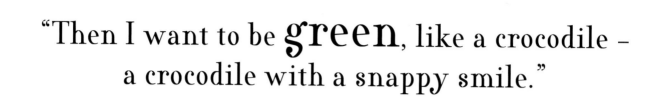

"Then I want to be **green**, like a crocodile –
a crocodile with a snappy smile."

"But penguins are not crocodiles.
You're black and white, and
you walk for miles."

"Then can I be **red**,
just like a fox –
with a bushy tail
and four black socks?"

"No, you're not red
or sly or cunning.
You're black and white,
and not made for running."

"Then I want to be **orange**,
like an orangutan –
an orangutan
in a jungle gang!"

"But a penguin can't live high in a tree.
You're black and white, and you'd miss the sea."

"Can I be **purple**, like a butterfly –
And fly with the birds up in the sky?"

"Penguins can't fly to and fro!
You're black and white, and you slide on snow."

"Then I'm going to be **pink**,
just like a pig –
with a curly tail and a belly so big!"

"But you're not pink and you don't like muck.
You're black and white, with feet like a duck."

"Can I be **brown**, like a fearsome bear –
a grizzly bear with a grizzly stare?"

"Pip, you're black and white
with a lovable stare,
and about as fierce as a teddy bear!"

"Then I'm going to be yellow,
like a big proud lion –
a lion that's brave and as strong as iron."

"But, Pip, you're not a yellow cat.
You're a black-and-white penguin. That is that."

"Look!" says Dad.
"It's Skunk and Zebra! Panda, too!
They're black and white, just like you!
What's so wrong with black and white?
We think black and white's all right!"

So, at last little Pip has learned to see
that being yourself is the way to be.